Stuck

LISSETTE E. MANNING

Stuck

To Mary.

TABLE OF CONTENTS

ACKNOWLEDGMENTS

Many thanks to **Elina Jaunalksne** for allowing me the use of her photograph. I appreciate it very much.

To **Elizabeth Ann West** – I wanted to formally thank you for helping me with the blurb for the book that we came up with on Twitter. I very much appreciate it. I also wish you success with the release of your own book soon and pray that all goes well for you always. I look forward to reading your book when the time comes. May God bless you, and your own, always and may He keep you all, as well. It's truly a blessing in getting to know you and I thank God for having met you.

To **Craig Hallam** and **Kerry Meacham** – I appreciate the valuable insights and suggestions that you've both given me on how to improve my work. I hope that I can reciprocate and offer you both the same in the future. It's truly a pleasure and I wish you both the many of blessings with your own works – both present and future. I'm honored to call you both friends.

To **Virginia Lee** and **Brea Essex** – I am honored to have met you both and appreciate the time you've taken to read my work. I am blessed to have you both in my life and I hope that God will bless you both in all that you do. Whatever you need, please don't hesitate to ask.

To **Alex** – Thank you for your patience, Sweetness. And for always putting up with me. I love you, kiddo.

To **Mary** and **Kiki** – I mention you both again

because I truly appreciate the insights and suggestions that you've offered me when reading my stories. I hope that some day I can return the favor somehow. Thank you for your friendship. I'm very honored to have met you both.

1. THE WILL TO SURVIVE

Wails of the dying cut the night like sirens, studded with the crack of gunfire and moonlight winking on speeding bullets. The smell of burning flesh and rubber wafted through the air; the stench sickening my senses. Everywhere I looked, signs of a decaying world hit me.

Derelict buildings sat silent on random corners, ghostly shells sporting broken windows and rotted wooden doors that hung off their hinges. Large cracks lined the road, stone and rubble littering the pavement. The shadows converged as I walked along the darkened streets, catching occasional glimpses of an abandoned car.

Mounds of tattered scraps of cloth and bone were strewn across the uneven terrain. The bodies were so singed that it was difficult to discern whether they were once male or female. My heart constricted as my gaze fell upon a small body that lay curled into a tight ball near the side of a building. Approaching with caution, I gasped. Her skin was charred in places, bits flaking off as a slight breeze began to pick up. Her arms were wrapped around the remnants of a teddy bear; her chin tucked between its glassy eyes.

Tears rose to the surface as I gazed upon the child. I yearned to know who she was and how she'd come to be there, yet her life would forever remain a mystery. This made me all the more determined to provide for my family.

An encounter such as this one was an every day occurrence here in Boise, Idaho. You would never know that this was once a very prosperous and quite popular city. The world we now lived in was a far cry from the one we'd known.

In the early days, we'd lived with the belief that the earth would end in a storm of fire and brimstone, anxiously waiting for a merciful God to take his people to the Promised Land. Days passed and nothing happened. Years sped on by without anything of consequence occurring. Eventually, we came to believe that perhaps we were wrong about everything that we'd believed in.

Yet the predictions were right. To some extent. Fire and brimstone did fall from the sky, but not as an act of God. It came in the form of a meteor cluster passing through our solar system. With their path off kilter, they'd tumbled through space obliterating everything at such an alarming rate that we were unprepared for the destruction.

STUCK

The impact took many lives. However, the world didn't end as we knew it. It left most of us in limbo, trying to survive. The scattered forces of the military had tried to establish order amidst the chaos, but their efforts were to no avail. Vandalism broke out. People fought with one another to find food and shelter; countless lives lost over the smallest of things.

An abandoned Victorian house sat at the end of the lane, a large, gaping hole spanning the length of its roof. Yanking the rusted gate open, I walked up the weather-beaten path, taking care to avoid the bits of glass, pieces of wood and crumbling stone that were haphazardly scattered about.

The front door had been pulled off of its hinges and now lay disintegrating at the bottom of the stone steps. Climbing over it, I made my way inside. The strong scent of decay hit my nostrils as I shoved a hand into one of my pockets and produced a small flashlight. Twisting its base, I waved it about; its weak beam of light falling across dusty puffs of cotton and moldering curtains.

A broken cardboard box lay at the foot of the stairs, most of its contents scattered across the floor. Marching towards it, I pulled its tattered lids apart and rummaged through it in hopes of finding something of value. The tip of my finger stung as I grazed it across bits of glass that lay at its bottom. Sucking on my finger, I tossed aside a moth-eaten book, its cover falling off as it landed on the floor.

This is how we live now. Like animals - paranoid and ill-at-ease, always looking over our shoulders as we scrounge about for something to eat.

James hadn't wanted me to go out in search of food to abate our hunger. His concern that vigilantes or some other rogue faction were bound to harm me was touching. I'd assured him that I would be fine, the need to provide for my children spurring me into action. The sweet sound of his voice rose to my ears as I recalled his subtle reprimand over the fact that I was ready to leave the sanctuary of our home.

James' eyes narrowed to half slits, his lips pursed. "Damn it, Annie! You don't have to do this. The kids will be fine."

"No," I said. "Food is almost non-existent. If we keep waiting for the military to bring us supplies, we'll die. It's been months since they kept their promise. I can't keep waiting."

Curling his hands into tight fists, he slammed them down upon the tabletop causing it to wobble slightly. "I can't let you go out there. You know what's waiting. You could be killed!"

Shaking my head at him, I stood my ground. "Yes, it's dangerous out there, but it's not as if I haven't done this before."

"I know that, woman!"

Wrapping my hands about his face, I pressed a desperate kiss upon his lips. "I'll be fine, darling. I promise."

He rubbed the palms of his hands across his haggard face, knowing that he would never win the battle that raged between us. "You'll come back?"

I blinked back the tears that threatened to spill down my cheeks as I kissed him once more. "Of course."

"I don't like this. Why don't I go instead?"

"You wouldn't know what to look for."

His nostrils flared with suppressed anger. "I can try, can't I?

STUCK

You're better off staying here with the children."

Stamping my feet against the floor, I refused to give in to his demands. "No, dearest. This is something that I must do. For the children. For you. For all of us!"

Hugging him to me, I breathed in his scent. He held on tight, his body shaking with the effort. I pulled away, risking a glance about the one-room cottage. My children's faces were forever branded into my memory. Blowing them kisses, I turned around and yanked the door open. A cold gust of wind hit me in the face as I stomped out into the night with hopes of providing for those I loved more than life itself.

Wiping the corner of an eye, the images of my children surfaced as I dug through the box; strengthening my resolve in hopes of finding something that would calm the aches within their bellies. Sammy's pale, wan face - his dull eyes peeking through those sunken sockets, beckoned me. I refused to disappoint him.

Lilly's trembling lips sang a song of despair every time she looked at me. I could not bear to come home empty-handed. They hung on to life by a thread, a slim chance of hope filling their hearts whenever I returned with an offering from the world outside. It was for them that I sacrificed the warmth and safety of my home.

Finding nothing of use within the box, I moved on. Instincts of survival were honed deep inside me as I crept along the darkened streets. A sudden burst of gunshots went off nearby, my neck cracking loudly as I whipped my head about in search of where it came from. My hackles rose as the shadows danced before my very eyes.

I narrowed them, refusing to give in to the panic that

threatened to consume me. I did not want to die out here. Not now. Not like this.

Curling my hands into tight fists, I weaved back and forth through the streets. Jumping over desiccated corpses and the occasional rubble, I dodged the bullets as they came closer. Running around a corner, someone shouted for me to stop.

"You!" said the voice, angry and rough around the edges. "Stop right there!"

I froze, squinting as I searched for the voice's owner. Yet the darkness kept me from finding its source. My chest tightened as fear began to seep through my veins. Death would come for me if I were to listen to the voice's pleas. I urged my body forward and continued on.

The ground shook beneath my feet as something crashed into a building nearby. Throwing myself onto the ground, I covered my head. Pieces of cement and wood rained down, several hitting me across the back, shoulders, and legs; places that were already sore from running.

Oh, God. Don't let me die. Please. Not now!

"Annie!" a voice whispered, catching me by surprise. "Over here."

The scent of smoke lifted into the air as the deteriorated wood within the building caught fire. The flames flickered to and fro, illuminating the small square as it began to spread. Raising my head, I caught sight of Winston Porter as he lay huddled against the side of the building. The right sleeve of his green shirt was torn, blood dripping from an uneven gash across his bicep.

STUCK

A severed arm lay several inches from my face, the fingers curled around the trigger of what used to be a rifle. The rest of the body was nowhere in sight. A sharp pain rent through me as I tried to pull myself forward. A jagged piece of wood pierced the center of my back, pinning me in place. Try as I might, I could not dislodge it.

Blood dribbled from my lips as I watched Winston sit up and extract a Swiss army knife from his pocket. Yanking off his shirt, he cut it into strips and bound the wound to keep it from bleeding further. Satisfied with his efforts, he pushed himself down and began to crawl in my direction.

I lay there panting; the raspy sound that spilled from my lips chilling me to the very bone. No matter how hard I tried, no words came forth. My body refused to cooperate. It was as if I had shut down completely, unable to wind the cogs that allowed my body to function. Darkness crept across my vision, blocking out the meager light and my hopes to survive.

2. CONSEQUENCES

My vision adjusted to a peeled, cracked ceiling as my eyes opened; the surroundings unknown to me. Where am I?

The thick scent of antiseptic stung my nostrils. Coarse cotton met my fingertips as I lay upon the bed. Cobwebs covered the corners of the wall as I measured its length with my sight. The cedar paneling that draped the left wall was chipped and slightly faded, dirt coating its edges.

Panic filled me as I willed my body to move. It simply refused to do what I was telling it to do. A hand pressed itself against my forehead. A face materialized before me, a sad smile playing about the woman's lips.

Was I dead? Perhaps that would explain the disconnected feeling that had begun to spread throughout my body.

STUCK

Images of what had happened were a little hazy, for I could only recall bits and pieces of the ordeal. Waging a war against my inner self, I tried to understand what was wrong. I couldn't move, nor could I hear. I could see, but couldn't speak. My sense of touch was intact, that much I knew, as my hands itched with the memory of the thick, coarse cotton of the sheets that covered the bed underneath me.

She rolled me onto my stomach, giving me a clear view of the room as she gently pulled my head to the side. I winced as her hands probed the tender area at the center of my back. A moan burst from my lips as she pulled the bandage from my skin. Memories fell into place as it dawned on me that Winston and I were not the only ones that had been caught in the crossfire. I wondered what had become of him.

Metal beds occupied every inch of the chamber. Some were empty. Others were occupied by writhing bodies that sought release from the pain that ravaged their bodies. Spots of red dotted their sheets, some spreading outward as they pulled against the bandages that were taped across a severed limb or those that held stitches into place.

An attendant rushed into my line of sight, pinning one of her patients across the bed as he tried to rise. His mouth opened wide in a silent scream as he flailed back and forth. The covers fell away to reveal the blackened, bleeding stumps of what had once been his legs. His fingernails dug into the side of the nurse's face as he lashed out at her, blood coursing down her cheek.

My vision blurred as the nurse rolled me around once more and pushed me down against the bed. She fluffed the pillow beneath my head, smoothing away the soft tendrils of hair that had fallen across my brow. Her gray eyes were full of pity as she pulled the blanket about my shoulders. I appreciated that she was making sure I was comfortable, but it did nothing to calm the dread within me.

Narrowing my eyes, I focused on the movement of her mouth. Frustration built as I saw her lips press into a tight line. Gently patting me across the shoulder, she moved away without a further glance in my direction.

She probably thinks that I'm a lost cause, but I'm not. I have no intention of kicking the bucket, I thought to myself.

I lay there brooding over the circumstances that had led to my current state of immobility. The force of the explosion might have caused my eardrums to rupture as I had fallen. I was certain that the impact of the wood against my back must have severed my spine and the nerves that allowed me to move about. It was the only logical explanation that I could think of.

Yet I was unable to discern as to why I could not speak. My throat felt as if it were intact, for I could feel myself swallow. Perhaps my vocal cords had been damaged somehow because of the bomb's detonation.

Another face came into focus, my heart racing with anticipation. I drank in the contours of James' face, slaking my thirst as I remembered the softness of his skin and the scent of musk and homemade lemon soap that permeated from its pores. My lips craved his as I recalled his tender kiss.

A sweet sense of longing filled me as images of the life we'd lived together surfaced. James wiping Sammy's bottom clean. His pulling Lilly across his lap and hugging her tight as he eased her fears about a nightmare that she'd had. Our bodies writhing in unison as we sought release from the ravages of feeling that consumed us as we made love.

The torn look within his eyes broke through my reverie, pulling upon the strings of my heart. My palms began to itch as I yearned to lift my arms and wrap them about him.

His knowing eyes searched mine for some sign that I was cognizant of my surroundings. Disappointment soon filled their dark depths as he sat down upon the edge of the bed. Wrapping his large hands around one of my own, he brought my hand up and gently grazed his lips across my knuckles. I kept my eyes rooted to the movement of his lips. An elderly man appeared beside him, a frown marring his face.

The doctor's crinkled, yet wizened, face peered down at me; concern filling the depths of his blue eyes. James appeared to ask a question. His lips soon pressed into a tight line. The doctor spoke, shaking his head. Glancing my way, the corners of James' mouth turned down as his nostrils flared with anger. They were oblivious to the fact that I could see them standing there above me. He nodded as the doctor pointed in my direction. His fingers gradually tightened about my hand.

I'm here, Darling, I thought. I'm here. I can see you!

He absently rubbed the pad of his thumb across the back of my hand as the doctor squeezed his shoulder and walked away. His gaze was turbulent as he reached down and curled his hand about by my cheek. A light sheen of moisture filled his eyes as he bent down to kiss my lips. His rancid breath fanned my face as he pressed his cheek against my own.

I began to weigh the implications of my folly, wondering if I would ever make it out of the void in which I now found myself. It bothered me that I could neither move, nor hear, nor speak.

If only, I thought. If only I had not ventured out that night. I would be home, safe and sound.

The urge to go out in search of nourishment had been too strong; my children's well-being my driving force. My search had proved unfruitful, cut short by an explosion that had almost obliterated everything around me.

And here I lay. Upon a bed in some God-forsaken place, not knowing whether I am whole or in pieces.

James shifted beside me, his cheeks wet from the tears that he'd shed for me. I committed to memory the color of his eyes, the curve of his cheeks, the outline of his lips, and the haphazard curl of hair that hung over his brow as he gazed down at me. The memory of him would remain with me forever.

My bosom swelled as the love that I held for this man surged forth. I had vowed to cherish him for the rest of my life and now wished that I had listened to his wisdom. That I had stayed home, instead of going out in search of something that I would never find.

Something drew my husband's attention, a deep scowl tarnishing the contours of his face. The mother in me ached to alleviate his worries. To hold him close and tell him that everything would be all right.

I hated this. Being stuck within a darkness that threatened to overwhelm me.

Will it ever go away? I wondered. Will I be able to hold my children again? To hear their sweet voices as they spoke? To feel their arms wrapped around me as I soothed away their fears?

Remorse filled me as I thought about him. About the children. I lamented that I had not listened to James in the first place. I wouldn't be here, if I had. I'd be home, my arms wrapped around my children.

Instead, I am locked inside myself. Unable to move or speak. Unable to tell the world that I am indeed here.

James leaned forward and brushed his lips against mine, the sorrow within his eyes tearing at the edges of my heart. The pain that he was feeling was my doing and there was nothing that I could do to ease it. His hand pressed softly against my own, his mouth a soft flutter against my skin as he uttered a goodbye that never reached my ears.

His shoulders slumped with defeat as he acknowledged that I would never be the same person that I had been before. Tears slid down his cheeks once more as he shook his head in denial. It was evident that he thought me lost to him. I had no way of showing him that it was not true, for I was a prisoner of my own making.

The anguish that was written upon his face cut me to the core. He pressed a kiss against my forehead, squeezing my shoulder as he straightened. He moved away from my bed, a blur of blues and greens on the edge of my periphery. And just like that, he was gone; leaving me alone.

Taking a deep breath, I allowed my tears to fall; the thin trails of salted water snaking down the length of my cheeks. Somehow, I knew that he was never coming back for me. Desolate and alone, I closed my eyes and spiraled towards the darkness that had finally come to claim me.

Sometimes, the will to live is the only thing we can hold on to.

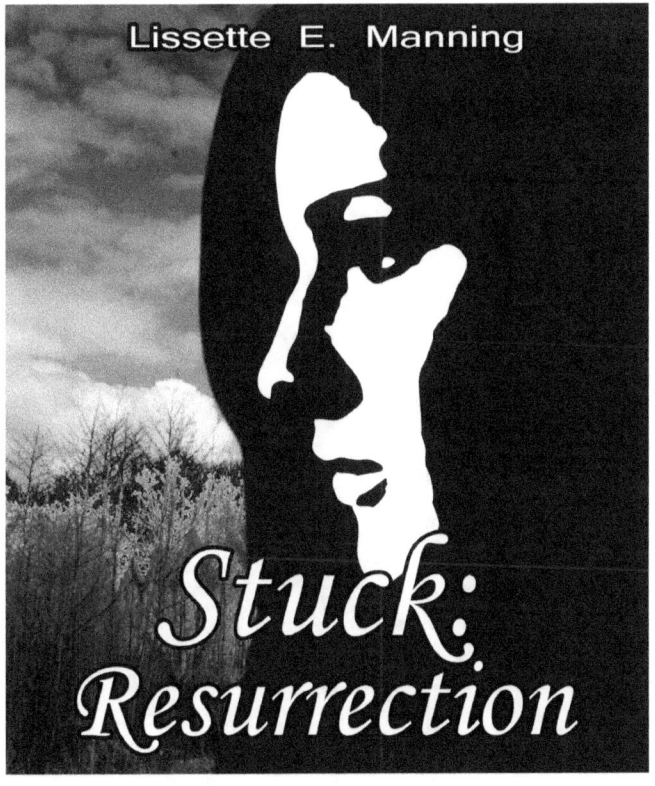

Enjoy an excerpt from *Stuck: Resurrection*, book 2 in the *Stuck* series.

CHAPTER 1

A PAINFUL BEGINNING

I awoke to darkness. My thoughts were scattered. Fear enveloped every inch of me. I willed myself to move, but my body refused to listen. A bed lay beneath me, that much I knew. The coarse linen pressed against my flesh, a stark reminder that I'd lain in bed for far too long.

Although my memory was far too hazy, bits and pieces of the past surfaced. I recalled the bombing, the excruciating pain, and James' face as he'd stared at me with pity deep within his eyes. He'd given up on me without giving me a chance to pull through my unexpected ordeal.

A sharp gasp escaped me as I soon moved my stiff limbs for the very first time. The encroaching darkness threatened to consume me, but I fought it at every turn. I'd come too far to give up now. One way or another, I would get up from the bed on which I lay.

Pain radiates through every inch of my body. My muscles, tendons, and rickety bones protested at the abuse, but I refused to give up. I'd been a prisoner of my own flesh for far too long. It was time for me to take the bull by its horns, and reclaim that which belonged to me once more.

Huffing and puffing from the effort, I felt my right leg give way. It slipped off of the bed, hanging loose over the side of it. I held my breath as I willed my other leg to move. Blood pulsed frantically through my veins, sweat erupting through my every pore.

My left leg twitched, and shifted slightly to the right. I released a pent-up breath as several hot tears seeped from the corners of my eyes. It felt good to move again, however little the movement was. I flexed my fingers, delighted to feel them jerk back and forth ever so slightly.

That's it, I told myself. Just a little more!

Little by little, I slid my stiff form toward the edge of the bed. With every push, I gained a little more confidence. From the sound of things, I was alone in this darkened place. Nothing else stirred around me.

I soon found myself curled upon the side of the bed, my legs and my left arm hanging off of its edge. Utilizing my right arm, I scooted closer to the edge with every small push. I fingered the ridge of the mattress with the fingers of my right hand, elated to have come so far in so short a time. The task was monumental for me after having lived within myself for so long.

Push, Annie, push! I urged myself. You can do it!

I flopped onto my stomach, my face pressed deep into the coarse linen. With a small nudge of my head, I turned my face so that I had a little room to breathe. My fingers brushed against the lower part of the mattress. With careful precision, I slid my legs further to the side. More tears streamed down my cheeks as my toes touched the floor.

Oh, my God! I thought. I'm doing it!

Push after small push, I was able to move my hips over the mattress's ridge. The unexpected momentum carried my entire body with it. I landed on the floor in a heap, the air rushing out of my lungs. Plumes of dust burst into the air, the particles pouring into my nose and mouth with every breath I took.

Oh, God! I don't want to die here. Please, don't let me die here!

Silence enveloped me as I lay there on the floor. I felt like a fish out of water, barely able to breathe. The encroaching darkness made it extremely difficult to see. It was hard to decipher as to whether I was still in the hospital, or if they'd moved me somewhere else. Nor did I know if there were others around.

Determined to not become a victim of my own making, I carefully worked my body around until I lay on my back. My limbs were still stiff, and they weren't responding to me completely, but they moved just enough to allow me the movement I was searching for. That, in itself, was surprising, considering that the blast had let me in a catatonic state. Previously, I'd assumed I would remain that way forever. Yet, here I lay, regaining my senses, albeit ever so slowly.

God was being merciful by giving me a second chance. I knew that now. I would make the most of it, and do right by my family once I got out of this hellhole. The first thing I'd do once I got a better hold of my body was to go home. I'd embrace my beautiful children, and make love to James, if he'd let me.

Those thoughts and more strengthened my resolve. I'd get out of this place soon enough. First, I needed to regain complete movement of my entire body. No matter how much it hurt, I'd get up, and walk again. My family was out there somewhere. They needed me, just as much as I needed them. Somehow, some way, I would see them once more.

ABOUT THE AUTHOR

Lissette E. Manning is an author from Connecticut. She has been writing since she was six-years-old, and enjoys giving life to the stories always brewing in her head. She enjoys reading, music, playing video games, spending time with friends and family, and is also a bit of a computer geek.

Connect With Her Online:

Email: lizziebeth1095@sbcglobal.net
Facebook:
http://www.facebook.com/LissetteElizabethManning
Twitter: http://www.twitter.com/xLizzieBethx
Website: http://www.simplistik.org
Blog: http://www.simplistik.org/lissetteemanning
PInterest: http://pinterest.com/gethsemane95
Goodreads:
http://www.goodreads.com/author/show/4867044.Lissette_E_
Manning